THE MAGIC
MOTH

THE MAGIC MOTH

by Virginia Lee
Drawings by Richard Cuffari

THE SEABURY PRESS · NEW YORK

Text copyright © 1972 by Virginia L. Ewbank
Drawings copyright © 1972 by The Seabury Press
ISBN: 0-8164-3043-8
Library of Congress Catalog Card Number: 73–171862

Design by Judith Lerner
Printed in the United States of America

Second Printing

for Lori Ann and my father

CHAPTER ONE

I<small>F, SOME</small> evening around 5:30, you were to take a walk down 128th Street, you would come to a gray house with "1205" over the front door. The grass in the small front yard is cut, but the edges are not trimmed. The paint is peeling, but not as badly as on some of the other houses on the street. This is an older neighborhood, and most of the people who live here cannot afford new paint for their houses as often as they need it.

If you looked through a window on the south side of

1205, you would see the George Foss family eating dinner around a brown, varnished, picnic-style table. George sits at one end in his comfortable old armchair. Irene, his wife, sits at the other end in a dining room chair with two red pillows on the seat and back.

On the bench at George's left is six-year-old Mark-O (for Mark Oliver) where Father can catch his milk when he spills it. Julie, nine, sits on her father's right by the kitchen door, so she can run for the sponge if Father misses.

Stephen, fifteen, sits next to Julie, but fairly near the middle of the table, where he can reach all the food. Barbie, fourteen, sits across from Stephen because that is the only place left.

Julie hates sitting where she does, because both Father's and Stephen's feet are big and she is always

getting tangled up with them under the table. It makes Stephen mad, and Father says, "Both of you keep your feet where they belong!" But no one ever says that to Father. Oh, no!

One evening the family was sitting as usual around the dinner table. It was the 27th of February, and they had just finished singing "Happy Birthday" to Augustus, the third guinea pig.

The Foss family has an interesting tradition, which did not come from anywhere. They started it themselves. They celebrate every birthday of every animal in the household just as they do their own. Since there are two dogs, an unknown number of cats who come and go, and four guinea pigs, there are several birthday cakes for dinner every month.

Frequently they get mixed up on the guinea pigs, and they have to make up the cats' birth dates, so it is likely that many of the animals get celebrated two or three times a year.

Whenever Mother is ready to bake a cake, she asks, "Whose cake is it to be this time?" If someone can remember an animal who has not had a birthday recently, there are candles on the cake that night.

The Fosses were starting on Augustus' chocolate marble cake with peppermint ice cream when Julie asked, "Hey! Whose birthday's next?"

"Maryanne's," Mother replied, putting a spoonful of the pink ice cream in a small dish.

"When is it?" asked Mark-O of anybody.

"Ninth of March," answered Stephen with his mouth full.

Mother got up from the table and took the dish of ice cream into Maryanne's room, just off the dining room. It has been over a year now since Maryanne, who is ten, last ate at the table with the family, or saw the tutor from school, or even got up out of bed. She has a heart defect.

Barbie, Julie, and Stephen take turns with Mother helping Maryanne eat her meals. They bring her little tidbits of the tenderest parts of the roast, or carefully buttered peas, or a bit of mashed potato dripping in gravy, and hold the plate while Maryanne takes a few bites. When she gets tired, they feed her the last of her food.

They also take turns thinking up special ways to decorate her portions of the meal. Sometimes Mark-O picks a little sprig of parsley for the potatoes (it grows wild under the kitchen window). Or Julie crumbles over a vegetable a piece of crisp bacon that she's saved from breakfast.

"I hope Maryanne wants green cake with peanut frosting for her birthday," screeched Mark-O after Mother had left the dining room.

Barbie looked at him severely. "Stop it, Mark-O. You know Maryanne can't eat cake. Momma will choose the cake, and you will like it or lump it."

Lately Barbie was acting more and more like a mother instead of a sister, and both Mark-O and Julie wished she'd change back. Mark-O decided to ignore her and turned to Father.

"Daddy, why can't Maryanne eat cake anymore? When can she?"

"Well," said Father slowly, "you know how sick she has been. That's why." He paused. "Perhaps she won't be able to eat cake, ever. Maybe she will have to go away soon."

"Where is she going?" asked Julie. "To the hospital again?"

Maryanne had been in the hospital for a long while when she was small, but when she came home she was not much better. Then, last year, a famous surgeon had operated on her heart. But afterward he had explained to Mr. and Mrs. Foss that there were some things doctors could not yet repair, and this was one of them.

"No—she won't be going to the hospital this time," said Father.

"I know what Daddy means," said Barbie. "He means Maryanne is going to die."

Everyone stopped eating. They were silent. You could

hear the hum of the electric clock on the wall.

Then Julie started to cry, and she put her napkin over her face.

Mother came out of the bedroom. She looked at Julie, then at the quietness of the others. Then she looked at Father. "Did you tell them?" she asked.

"Yes," he nodded. He took the big storybook with the green cover from the bookcase and went into Maryanne's room.

CHAPTER TWO

MARK-O got down on his hands and knees and crawled into the bedroom after Father. He thought that if he pretended he was a cat no one would notice. No one did. He wanted to look at Maryanne when she didn't know he was looking. He wanted to see if she really looked like someone who was going to die.

William Guinea Pig had died last summer, and Mark-O had cried, and they had buried it and got Mark-O a new one. It looked exactly like the one that died. But when

Mark-O looked at Maryanne, he thought, "I don't see how we could find another Maryanne." He felt terrible.

Father was reading about a princess named Proserpine, who was stolen away by a wicked king in a cave deep under the ground. The whole world was so sad that the trees lost their leaves and the grass dried up, and snow lay all over the earth. Later, Proserpine got to come back for half a year, and the green things grew again.

"And that," finished Father, "is why we have spring and summer and fall and winter."

For some reason, the story made Mark-O feel better. Maybe if Maryanne died and went away, she would come back. He went out to the living room to find Julie. Julie was his favorite relative. She didn't mind noise, she liked throwing things around and making messes, and she was always cheerful.

Mother was on the phone in the study, and Barbie was stacking dirty dishes.

"Barbie, where's Julie?"

"She's in the bathroom. She locked herself in and won't come out."

Mark-O went over to the door.

"Hey—leave her alone!" Barbie said. "She'll come out when she wants to."

Mark-O stomped up to his own room, which he shared with Stephen. The lights were out and there were just the lights from the hall. Stephen was sitting on the edge of his bed, his chin in his hands. He was thinking about Maryanne and how she always listened to him tell about football practice, even though she didn't know how to play.

There was a crayon line down the middle of the room, which Stephen had drawn three weeks ago.

"Mark-O," Stephen had said, "your side is over there, and mine is over here. If you get one toy on my side, I will disappear it! There's a secret hole under my bed. I'll drop the toy down it, and it will go clear through to China."

Mark-O tried to be careful, but one day two weeks ago his best orange ball had gotten over the line and disappeared. When he told Mother what Stephen had done with the ball, Mother had just smiled and said she was sure it would turn up.

Now, as Mark-O stood in the doorway looking at the line, he saw his orange ball, lying exactly within it on his side.

"My ball! Stevie, you got it back. How did you get it?" Mark-O cried.

"Well, I'll tell you, Mark-O, that ball was such a good ball that when I dropped it down the hole it bounced back up. It was so far to China that it took a whole week to go down and a whole week to bounce back." Stephen was smiling in an odd way.

"It did?" Mark-O's eyes were big. He could hardly believe such an amazing thing.

"Stevie, Maryanne will come back too, won't she?"

Stephen's smile disappeared and he didn't answer right away. When he did his voice sounded crackly as it often did lately. Father said it was because he was growing up.

"Well, no, she won't. But where she is going it will be nice."

"Is she going to China?"

"Creepers! Don't you know anything? Of course she's not going to China. When people die they go to heaven."

"Is heaven under the ground?"

"Of course not. Quit asking questions."

Mark-O took his ball and went back down to the kitchen. Mother was washing dishes and Barbie was drying. "Momma, can I give Maryanne a present for the guinea pig's birthday?"

"Of course, if you want to."

"What are you going to give her?" Barbie asked.

"My China ball," Mark-O answered, running off.

"Your what?" she asked, but he was already gone.

He ran into Maryanne's room. Father was giving her a drink of water, and she was sitting up part way on her pillows.

"Maryanne, guess what? Today was Augustus' birthday, and I got a present for you. Want it?"

Maryanne was sleepy, but she smiled and nodded. She liked Mark-O's presents. Nearly every day he brought her a bug in a jar or a pretty rock from the driveway or a drawing of something he saw going by on the street in front of the living room windows.

Last fall he had brought her a brilliant red and green caterpillar which had woven a cocoon. The jar stayed by her bed, and every day she expected to see a butterfly come out. Lately she had left the lid off so that the butterfly could get out when it was ready.

Before Maryanne had to stay in bed, she would often sit on the porch or on a blanket in the back yard, looking

at small things near her. She made up stories about them for Mark-O, who loved stories even when they had no ending or middle, and Maryanne's stories often had only a beginning.

After Mark-O began bringing presents to her, she still made up stories about them, but in the last few weeks she would only say, "I'm too tired," when he asked for one.

Now she held out her hands for the present and Mark-O put the ball in them. "It's pretty orange," she said. "That's your best ball. I thought Stephen put it down his China hole."

"He got it back. Guess what? It was such a good ball, it bounced back—all the way from China. It took one week to go and one week to come back. All the way under the ground. It's really special now."

Maryanne looked at it and rolled it around between her fingers. "It even feels different. I wish I could go all the way to China and come back, and I wouldn't be sick anymore." She closed her eyes.

"What do . . . ?" Mark-O started to ask, but Father shushed him.

"That was a very nice present, Mark-O," he said. "You were generous to give Maryanne your best ball. Maybe she can put it under her pillow and have a dream about it. Kiss her good night now. It's bedtime."

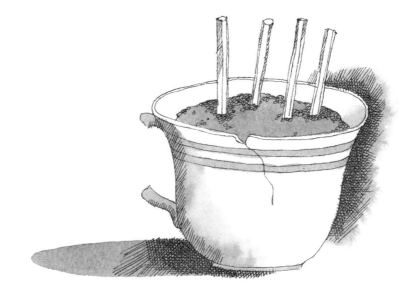

CHAPTER THREE

Next morning there were fresh grapefruit for breakfast, and new sharp metal spoons to eat them with.

"I got them with a tea coupon, and the grapefruit were ten for a dollar at the sale yesterday," Barbie announced. She was learning how to plan food-buying in her ninth grade home economics class, and had been doing much of the grocery shopping since Maryanne got so sick.

"The spoons are so Momma doesn't have to cut all the sections for us," Barbie said. "Look, you do it like this."

She showed everybody how to use the spoons, but it was hard the first time and before long there was juice all over everything. Mark-O's mess was the worst, but nobody criticized him. Father just said, "You'll get the hang of it after a while."

While Mark-O was working with his grapefruit, he found something. "Look, Barbie, it's a funny seed."

"It's awful big, all right," said Barbie. "My seeds are big, too."

"But look, its got a tail on it."

"Oh." Barbie stopped eating and looked closer. "Mark-O, that's a plant coming out of it! See the little leaves starting at the end?"

"Plant it, Mark-O," Julie urged. "It will grow a grapefruit tree."

"Momma, can I plant it?"

"Yes. After breakfast. Eat now. Your eggs are getting cold."

After breakfast, Barbie grabbed her lunch and ran for her jacket and books.

"Brush your teeth!" called Father.

"I can't, I'm going to miss my bus," called Barbie as she slammed the door.

"Darn!" exclaimed Julie. "She's always copping out on the breakfast dishes!" Julie's bus came an hour later than Barbie's and she was expected to clear the table and stack the dishes, but Barbie was *supposed* to help. When she couldn't, Mark-O got tagged for the job.

Mark-O ran for the bathroom. It was the safest place to be when it was time to clear the table. He locked the door. He'd show Julie she wasn't the only one who could hole up in there when people wanted her.

When he couldn't hear dishes clattering any longer, he flushed the toilet and made a noise with the water faucet, which rumbled when you turned it on a certain way. Sauntering out to the kitchen, he asked Mother, "Can we plant the seed, now?"

"Right now," she said, putting the last bowl in the dish drainer.

Just then, Stephen rushed through the kitchen, grabbed his lunch, whooshed through the door and slammed it behind him. Shortly after, Julie walked slowly in. She looked at the clock, grabbed her jacket and yelled, "I didn't know it was that late!" and slammed the door behind her.

Mark-O felt confused. Whenever he started something ten different things happened all at once, and he never got to finish.

"Boy, I'm glad they're all gone!" he sighed.

"Yes, I suppose you must be," answered Mother. "Now, take this old cup outside and fill it with dirt."

Mark-O went out on the front porch, slamming the

door like the others. He scooped up a cupful of dirt from the flower bed by the porch. Underneath the azalea bush he could see the little stick with the paper on it that said, "William Guinea Pig." The dirt was cold and wet and heavy. "That's an awful place for William to be," Mark-O said to himself as he went back inside.

"Momma, do you think William is cold out there?"

"No, I don't," she answered.

"Why?"

"Well, because after guinea pigs die, they don't feel anything anymore."

"Are you sure?"

"I am very sure."

"Is that what will happen to Maryanne?"

"Yes," said Mother slowly, "but that is only part of what will happen. That is the least important part."

"What else will happen?"

Mother sighed. "Did you ever go to sleep and dream you were someplace else?"

"I did once when I dreamed I was in an airplane flying over the ocean."

"I remember that night, too. You kicked your covers off and got cold. I came in and covered you up. Do you remember that?"

"No."

"Did you know that you were in your bed and that you were cold?"

"No. I really thought I was in the airplane."

"That's a little bit like what will happen to Maryanne. She will go to sleep and not know she is here. The important part of her, that does the dreaming, will be someplace else."

"Oh." Mark-O felt better.

"Let's put your seed in the dirt now," said Mother. "In fact, let's put three or four of these seeds in, and stick a match by each one to mark it. We'll see which one comes up first."

Mark-O punched a hole for each seed with the match, and dropped in the seed. Then he lit four matches over the sink and blew them out. He put a match beside each seed and pressed down the dirt.

Mark-O picked up the cup and went into Maryanne's room. She was lying very still. Her eyes were almost closed, but she was not asleep because when she heard him she opened her eyes and turned her head.

"I'm glad you're not asleep," Mark-O said. "Look, I planted four grapefruit seeds, and I'm having a contest to see which one comes up first."

Maryanne was silent for a while, then she said very softly, "What will you give the seed that comes up first?"

Mark-O was puzzled. He hadn't thought of that. "I know, I'll give the seed to you."

"Okay," Maryanne said, and closed her eyes.

Mark-O huffed. "Why do you always have to go to sleep when I'm talking to you?" When Maryanne didn't stir, he ran back to the kitchen.

"Momma! I think Maryanne went to sleep! Is she all right?"

Mother seemed a little upset. "Look, Mark-O, don't worry if Maryanne goes to sleep. It's good for her. And please don't talk to Maryanne about it."

"Don't you want her to know?"

"She already knows, but I don't want her to worry about going to sleep." She put her hands on his shoulders. "Mark-O, this is a very hard time for all of us. We will talk about it some more later, all right?"

Mother looked tired. What is more, she said, "I'm tired. You go get ready for school now."

Mark-O's kindergarten class was in the morning and he got home for lunch every day. He put the cup with the grapefruit seeds in it on the kitchen windowsill and ran to get his jacket.

CHAPTER FOUR

ALL THAT WEEK, things went on as they always had. Julie was almost late for her bus every morning, and Barbie missed hers once and had to walk. Every night they argued over who cleared the table. Every morning, Mark-O fed the guinea pigs and looked to see if the seeds had come up, and every night he asked Stephen a million questions about China and other things that were on his mind. The seeds never came up, and he was never satisfied with Stephen's answers. Most of the time Stephen would say, "I dunno. I guess you better ask Dad."

Sometimes, Mark-O thought, big brothers are the stupidest people in the world. When he said so to Father, Father just smiled and remarked, "Perhaps the feeling is mutual."

In between times, Mark-O took his endless stream of worms and leaves and empty pill bottles and loose glass beads that had rolled under the furniture in to Maryanne. He was increasingly disappointed because she was asleep so much, and when she was awake, she didn't say much to him.

"What's the matter?" he asked one afternoon when she did not smile at one of his presents. "Don't you feel good?"

"No." Maryanne closed her eyes tight and would not say anything more.

Mark-O went to find Mother. "Momma, Maryanne doesn't feel so good. You better give her a pill."

"I can't do that just now," she said. "I already did give her one." Then she went into Maryanne's room and shut the door.

Mark-O knew that when Mother did that he was absolutely not to go in after her. He didn't like being shut out. What was going on in there? His stomach began to hurt. Finally, he went to look at his seeds for the second time that day. Still, nothing. Angrily he dug down with his finger and found one of the seeds. He put it in the palm of his hand. The seed was nearly black, and it crumbled into several pieces. It seemed to be all dried up.

Just then, Barbie came in from school and saw him. "What did you do that for?" she asked. "If you dig your seeds up they won't grow."

"They won't anyway. Look at this—it's all ruined! It's dead!"

"No, it's not. All the seeds look that way right now. No! Don't dig them all up!"

Mark-O stopped just before he had emptied the whole cup out on the counter. "How do you know they are all that way?"

"Because I've grown more seeds than you ever will, and dug up lots of them when I was little. They all looked that way. You want plants, you take my word for it."

"But why?"

"I don't know. But the outsides of the seeds have to dry up and fall apart so the plants inside can grow."

"Is that what happens to all seeds?"

"It is if you plant them."

Mark-O put back the cup on the windowsill and went out on the porch. He sat down to wait for Julie. Presently she came running up the walk from the bus stop, all out of breath. That was the way she went everywhere—in a rush.

"What are you doing, Mark-O?" she asked cheerfully. "You look awful serious."

"I'm thinking."

"You? What are you thinking about?"

"I'm thinking I'd like to dig up William and see if he was going to grow into a plant. But I don't dare because if I did and he were, he wouldn't anyway."

Julie rolled her eyes and made a long face. "Goodness, Mark-O, you wouldn't want to do a thing like that. There wouldn't be much of anything left and besides it would look awful and besides that he won't make a plant anyway. Let's go have a snack."

"Why wouldn't there be anything left?"

"Because, if you bury something it just becomes part of the ground after a while."

Mark-O's stomach still hurt and he didn't want a snack. He started to stomp upstairs, but Barbie came out of the study and said in a fierce whisper, "You keep quiet! Maryanne's *very* sick. I have just called the doctor for Mother, and you are to *be quiet*."

Mark-O looked at her and thought, "You don't have to be so cross." Out loud, he said, "You aren't my boss." But anyway he tiptoed over to the davenport and sat down.

"I'm sorry, Mark-O," said Barbie. "I didn't mean to jump on you, but really, you don't have to stomp all the time. It's just as easy to walk."

"What's going on in Maryanne's room?" he asked.

"I don't know," Barbie answered.

Why is it that all the important things happen under the ground or behind closed doors? Mark-O wondered.

Julie was sitting on the dining room bench and he could just see her through the door. She wasn't eating her snack. Barbie sat in the easy chair and said nothing. She was frowning and biting on a nail.

After a long while, the doorbell rang.

"I thought doctors didn't come to houses," Julie said. "Before, we always took Maryanne."

"This is special," answered Barbie as she went to the door. She opened it for a man in a black overcoat, carrying a bag.

"This is the room, over here," she said, taking his coat and pointing to the door.

The man stopped and looked at Mark-O and Julie and asked them their names. "I'm Doctor Turner," he said. "I'll come back out and talk to you in a few minutes." Then he entered the bedroom, closing the door behind him.

In a few minutes he came out again, and Mother followed. Julie and Barbie had joined Mark-O on the davenport, and Dr. Turner sat down with them.

"Maryanne won't be with us much longer," he said. "Perhaps she will leave today." He said it in such a normal tone of voice that he might have been talking about Maryanne going on an ordinary trip.

"Why don't you take her to the hospital and make her well?" Julie asked. She almost sounded angry.

"Well," the doctor answered, "we have tried everything, including surgery, which you are old enough to remember. There is nothing else that *can* be done. Maryanne has been growing bigger all the time, and her heart is not strong enough to keep pumping for her as it did when she was small. And she is happiest in her own home, don't you think?"

"Ye-e-s," answered Julie.

"Can I go see her?" asked Mark-O.

"Yes, go ahead."

HOLDEMAN CHURCH PROPERTY

The doctor turned to Mother and said, "The medication I gave her should last for quite a while. She probably won't need any more. If you want me, just call. I'm off duty the rest of the day."

He left and Barbie and Mark-O and Julie all three went into Maryanne's room. They stood and looked at her, but all three felt too strange to say a word. Maryanne seemed to be asleep but they could hear her breathing in short, sharp breaths. Just then, she opened her eyes and smiled at Mark-O.

"Do you feel better, now?" he asked.

Maryanne nodded sleepily.

Mother said, "The doctor gave her something better than a pill. Now she feels much better."

So did Mark-O and he left the room. Just then Father came in early from the accounting office where he worked. He had a grocery bag that he handed to Barbie. It was full of TV dinners.

"Please start the oven and put these in," he said to her. He took off his coat and went into the bedroom. Julie came out and he shut the door.

Julie set the table, and when the oven was hot, Barbie put in the dinners. Neither one said a word, and Mark-O, who was full of questions, could not think just exactly what it was he really wanted to know, so he too was quiet.

Stephen came in from basketball practice. "I'm hungry," he announced. "What's for supper—TV dinners? You've got to be kidding!"

"Never mind—there's two for you, big boy," said Barbie, who thought his appetite was disgusting. She was secretly hungry all the time, herself. But she was afraid she was going to get fat, so she never ate much at the table.

"Why TV dinners? Is Momma sick or something?" Stephen wondered.

"No, Maryanne is worse. The doctor was just here. He thinks . . ." Barbie's words seemed to stick in her throat, and she didn't finish.

"She's going to go away tonight," said Mark-O, who had found his tongue again.

"Really?" asked Stephen in a whisper.

"Really," said Barbie.

Stephen, who never said much, said nothing now. He walked around the room trying to decide whether to go upstairs and take a shower or go in the living room and turn on the TV. Finally he turned on the TV very softly, but didn't look at it. Mark-O went in and sat down beside him in the easy chair.

"Do you feel bad, too?" he asked.

"Yeah, I feel awful." Stephen's voice cracked and went clear down in his chest.

37

CHAPTER FIVE

Wᴴᴇɴ ʙᴀʀʙɪᴇ called the family to dinner, Stephen discovered he was not hungry anymore. Neither was anyone else, so Barbie cleared away the half-empty aluminum plates and put Stephen's extra dinner in the icebox. Julie gave the leftovers to the dogs.

About eight o'clock, Barbie said, "Mother, it's time for Mark-O and Julie to go to bed."

"Never mind, Barbie," Mother replied. "They can stay up later tonight."

Julie and Mark-O felt an uncomfortable twinge. Some-thing very unusual had to happen before they could stay up. During the next hour Father read them two stories, and they played a game of checkers, which Julie was teaching Mark-O. Barbie and Stephen were trying to study, but they seemed nervous and jumpy.

"Julie, what do you suppose is going to happen?" Mark-O asked.

"I don't know," she answered.

A few minutes later, Father came out of the bedroom and said, "I think you should come in and say good-bye to Maryanne, now."

They all went in and stood around the bed. Maryanne looked just as she had before dinner. But there was a strange feeling in the room. It was like the feeling you get in your stomach when you are waiting for the dentist, only it wasn't just in their stomachs. It seemed to be all around.

One by one, each of the children went up and kissed Maryanne on the cheek. No one told them to. It was as if they knew what to do. First Barbie, then Stephen, then Julie, then Mark-O.

The room was very warm, but when Mark-O kissed Maryanne, her cheek felt quite cool. "Good-bye," he said inside himself. He was sure that he heard her answer, "Good-bye, Mark-O," inside herself. Then he thought she opened her eyes a crack and looked at him. The tiniest smile curled at the corner of her mouth.

He went back to the foot of the bed. It was so silent you could hear Maryanne's breathing, even though it was very soft now. Mark-O thought everyone else had stopped breathing, and he even thought he had. Suddenly, Maryanne was not breathing either.

For a long time, for many minutes, it was quiet. Then, all of a sudden, sound turned back on. Mark-O could hear the usual creakings and noises, the cars outside, the dogs barking, the refrigerator motor starting up. He felt as though he had waked up from a dream—almost.

Everyone moved slowly, like statues that had become alive. A huge white moth rose gently from somewhere near the bed and flew up to the ceiling. It fluttered around for a few seconds, found the window, which Mother had just opened, and glided out into the night. Mark-O watched it go.

Later, in the kitchen, Mother boiled water and made big mugs of instant cocoa. Her eyes were red from crying. She poured a little cream in the cocoa to cool it down, and dropped marshmallows in—two big ones in each cup. Father put bread in the toaster and got out the butter. Then he called Julie, who had locked herself in the bathroom again. She had been crying too, but she came out and sat down at the table with everyone else.

"Go ahead and cry, honey, if you want to," Father said. "You'll have plenty of company. But drink some cocoa, anyway, it will feel good."

Mark-O wanted to cry too, but he looked at Stephen first. He wondered if Stephen would, but he didn't. So Mark-O didn't either. But he started to shake all over, inside and out, and he couldn't stop.

Father sat him on his lap and put cocoa in front of him. "How about a piece of toast, Mark-O?" he asked.

The cocoa was comforting, and pretty soon Mark-O was not shaking anymore. The room was warm and all the lights were on. The group around the table seemed smaller than usual, but it was very close. The emptiness and the lonely feeling were, for the moment, left back in the bedroom, which Mark-O did not want to think about. For some reason, he was just terribly, awfully, unexplainably glad that they were all there in the dining room around the table.

Later, in his bed, Mark-O cried until his pillow was wet. It lasted a long time. Sometime before he went to sleep, he heard a car pull up, the door open and shut, and some people come up the walk. There was talking and moving around downstairs for quite a while, and somebody left, and more people came. Finally he went to sleep.

CHAPTER SIX

WHEN MARK-O came down to breakfast it was late, and Julie pulled him into a corner and whispered, "We don't have to go to school today. And do you know what? Maryanne is not in her bedroom. You ask Momma why. Okay?"

"No. She went away," said Mark-O. Then he remembered it wasn't that kind of going away. But he didn't want to ask Mother any more than Julie did.

They went to the table and neither one talked all

through the meal. They were worried. Mother did not talk, either. Her eyes were still red and puffy, and she sighed every few bites. Barbie and Stephen did not come to the table at all.

After breakfast, Mark-O tried to look into Maryanne's room without anyone watching him.

"I wonder if she is really gone," he said to himself. "Maybe it didn't really happen and she is still there and awake."

He stood in the door and looked at the empty bed and remembered all over again what had happened the night before. Only now it was even more like a dream. He looked at the caterpillar jar—the cocoon was cracked open. Going closer, he saw that it was empty. So that was where the white moth came from!

"Want to talk about something, Mark-O?" asked Father from behind him.

Mark-O jumped. "Ye-e-es. Where . . .?"

"She is at the funeral home, Mark-O. She will stay there until day after tomorrow, and then there will be a funeral. Right now, you and I are going shopping for groceries because there will be people coming to visit."

They bought bags and bags of groceries and when they got home, Aunt Shelley from Salt Lake City was there. Mark-O had seen her only once before in his life, two Christmases ago. Aunt Shell was cleaning and cooking

and talking all at once as fast as she could, which was fast.

In the afternoon, the minister from their church four blocks away came to call. Aunt Shell served coffee and cookies and everyone sat in the living room. First the minister talked to Mother and Father about the funeral service and what music they wanted and a number of things that Mark-O did not listen to. Then he asked everyone to bow his head while he said a prayer. "Father in Heaven, comfort Julie and Mark-O and Barbie and Stephen and their parents with the knowledge that life never ends—it just changes. Amen."

"Is that really true?" Mark-O asked him.

"That is what *I* believe," replied the minister. "I believe that when people die they step through a door into another place that we can't see with our eyes."

"Could they go through a window, too?" asked Mark-O, remembering the moth.

"Yes. Windows let in light, and I believe there is light where people go. But not the kind of light you see with your eyes. It is more like the kind you feel inside when you love someone, like Maryanne."

After the minister left, friends of Mother and Father came. Many were neighbors, most of whom had never been inside the Foss house before. It seemed to Mark-O and Julie that suddenly the family had a large number of friends that they had not known about. Everybody got served coffee and cookies.

The next day Mark-O, Julie, Barbie, and Stephen all went to school. Mark-O was glad. All those people and all that talking had begun to bother him. When he got out on the playground at recess, he ran faster, yelled louder, and played harder than he had ever done before. When he went home he was happy until he got to his porch. There were more people in the house! How he hated all these people! It was his house. Why wouldn't they leave him alone? He could hear them laughing, too.

He went in and stomped loudly up the stairs. When Mother called him down to lunch, he did not answer. She came up after him, but when she saw how angry he looked, she sat down on the bed with him and asked him what was the matter.

"Why don't you tell those people to go home? I can't play the record player and I can't get out the game box and I can't beat my drums and I can't. . ."

"Mark-O, don't you know why all these people are here?"

"They want to talk and laugh and make noise. Anyway, they shouldn't be laughing when Maryanne is dead." Mark-O started to cry.

"Mark-O, you must try to understand. These people are our friends. It is because they are our friends that they are here. They really feel as sad as we do, but they're able to think of cheerful things to say when we can't."

Mark-O tried to understand, because he wanted to please Mother. It was not easy, but then he remembered how comforting it had been sitting around the table drinking cocoa the night Maryanne left, and how glad he had been for his family then. He remembered, too, how this very morning he had laughed and played at school.

"Okay, Momma, it's all right for you to enjoy your friends. But I don't have to, do I?"

"No," said Mother, "but you should come down and enjoy your lunch, anyway."

CHAPTER SEVEN

NEXT MORNING, none of the children went to school. There was a heavy feeling in the house, as though something strange was about to happen.

They all got dressed in their best clothes and sat in the living room, waiting for the time to go to the funeral. Mark-O's stomach was hurting again. He had never been to a funeral and he *knew* he would not like it. The night before, Julie had whispered to him that this was when they would bury Maryanne in the ground. He remembered how cold the ground was this time of year and it worried him.

"Do I have to go?" he asked Mother.

"Yes, you do," she replied firmly. "Anyway, it will not last very long. You will feel better if you go. Remember how you always bury guinea pigs when they die? You read poems when you put them in the ground, and you say a prayer. Then you feel better. This will be like that."

Mark-O looked at Stephen to see how he felt. "I don't like getting dressed up, either, but we have to be men, you know," Stephen said.

Mark-O was puzzled to see a smile appear on Father's face, as though Stephen had said something funny. But he decided he had better act at least as grown-up as Stephen.

Father looked at his watch and got up. There was a vase of tiny white rosebuds on the coffee table. Father handed one bud to each of the children. "Take good care of them," he said. "You will need them later."

They put on their coats and walked together down the street to the church. Inside, the organ was playing. An usher took them to a front section of seats which had been roped off with a red silk cord. He let them in and removed the cord. Other people were coming in the back. Mark-O saw many whom he knew—there was even the principal of his school, where Maryanne had gone too, but only for half days in the first grade.

Then Mark-O looked at the front of the church. There were more flowers than he had ever seen in one place. And there was a strange white box right in the middle in front of the altar. It had a blue cloth over it. Mark-O was going to ask what was in it, but he had the uncomfortable feeling that he knew.

The organ stopped playing and the minister, who now had a long black robe on, got up to speak. He talked about Maryanne and Mark-O tried to listen. It wasn't easy. The air in the church was stuffy, and besides his right leg was going to sleep. When he wriggled it, Aunt Shell gave him a stern look.

Then the minister read long passages out of the Bible. They were hard to understand because of the long words. Finally there was a prayer and the minister sat down again.

Father got up and motioned to the children to follow him. They filed out of the church and were put into the station wagon of a friend of Father's. Mother and Aunt Shell got in with them, but Father went off and got into a long, very black car at the side of the church. Mark-O could see several men carrying the white box out and putting it into the back of the black car. By that time, all of the people had left the church, and the black car started down the driveway. The station wagon pulled out right after it. Mark-O could see the other cars following them.

"That's a *hearse*," whispered Julie, who had been to a funeral before. "All the people follow it to the graveyard with their lights on."

"Why?" asked Mark-O.

"So people will know this is a funeral and will let all the cars go together even if there is a red light."

Mark-O had the strange feeling that everything that was happening was part of a Big Law that had to be obeyed. You could see all these unpleasant things getting ready to happen, but you couldn't keep them from happening. Even if you could, he guessed you wouldn't, because you would have to stay behind while the rest of the family went on and that would be worse.

"I wish I could run away," he whispered to Julie.

"Me, too," agreed Julie, "except I want to put my rose on the coffin."

Mark-O looked at his rose. The stem was bent in one place and it looked wilted because he had held it inside his hand too long.

"What's it for?" he asked Julie.

"We put it on the coffin before it's buried—it's like giving it to Maryanne."

"Oh."

When the cars arrived at the cemetery, the people followed the family to a place where a hole had been dug.

A huge pile of dirt was beside it, covered with a green plastic cloth. Some men carried the coffin over and set it down next to the hole, and removed the blue cloth. The minister stood beside it and the family gathered around. He opened a little book and began to read.

"Dust to dust, earth to earth . . . ," he read.

"Is that what you meant about William being part of the ground?" Mark-O whispered to Julie.

"I guess so," said Julie.

". . . We commend her spirit to Heaven and her body to the earth from whence it came," finished the minister.

Father whispered to the children, "Now you may go over and put your roses on the coffin if you wish to."

Mark-O, Stephen, and Julie, and Barbie together placed their roses on the coffin. Four men carefully let the

coffin down into the hole and some other men took the green cover off the dirt.

Mother took Mark-O's hand and went to the station wagon, followed by the rest of the family. Barbie, Julie, and Mother cried all the way home, and Father sat in the front seat alone, not talking to anyone, even the friend who was driving. Stephen sat with Mark-O in the little second back seat where there was only room for two. Mark-O stuck his hand in Stephen's pocket and looked out the window. Stephen put his arm around Mark-O, and they looked out the window together.

CHAPTER EIGHT

ALL THE children went back to school the next day and Father went back to work at his office. Aunt Shell left with Father, who was to drop her off at the bus station so she could go home to her job. The funeral seemed like something that had happened last year instead of yesterday.

The house was still and empty. Mark-O did not have to leave for two hours. Again, he had the feeling that if he went into Maryanne's room she would be there. He walked by and looked in the door, but of course she wasn't. He went out onto the porch, hoping he might see something interesting. But there was no Maryanne to take it to, even if he found something. He went back inside and sat on the davenport.

Mother came in with the vacuum cleaner. The rug was a mess after all the company.

"Well, Mark-O," she said, "you are very quiet today. Is something wrong?"

"I just want Maryanne back."

"Yes, I know," sighed Mother, sitting down beside him. "We all miss her." She gave him a hug.

"Why did she go away?"

"That is something I don't know for sure, Mark-O, but some people do not seem to be meant to live very long."

"Then why was Maryanne born?"

Mother thought for a while before she answered. "Maryanne was very happy in our family. Everyone was good to her and she was someone very special. You did not give anyone else presents every day, did you? And you did not walk quietly in anyone else's room because they were sleeping. But lately I have noticed that you are learning to be more thoughtful of other people as well."

Mother ruffled Mark-O's hair. "We all learned many things from Maryanne," she said. "Mostly, I guess, how much we appreciate our family."

Mark-O was pleased—he *did* understand what Mother was saying.

Mother smiled. "Maryanne was like the plants in our garden," she said. "They only last a short while, but they make us happy while they are here."

That reminded Mark-O of something. "Momma! I forgot all about my seeds! Did you water them?"

"Yes, and I forgot to tell you this morning, but something is happening to them."

Mark-O ran to the kitchen. One plant was already up, with two fat green leaves. Another was just breaking the surface—a little mound cracked open at the top revealed a piece of green leaf curled up inside. The larger plant had a piece of the old seed fastened to it. The seed was black and crumbly like the one he had dug up.

"Oh, Momma!" Mark-O called. "I promised the first plant to Maryanne. It didn't come up in time!"

"Don't feel too badly about that," said Mother, following him into the kitchen. "When it gets bigger we can plant it outside and call it our 'Maryanne Tree.'"

That would be nice, thought Mark-O. Maybe the white moth would come and sit in it. "When will it grow bigger?" he asked.

"Perhaps next year, if you water it well," answered Mother.

A year was too long. "I want to do it *now,*" Mark-O

said, loudly and clearly.

"The plant isn't ready. You'll have to take care of it until it is," Mother explained.

An idea was stirring inside Mark-O, but he didn't know what it was, yet. There was something he wanted to do. Something for Maryanne?

He stood on one foot, looking at the tiny tree. He was thinking about it growing tall as the house. Inside his mind he could see its branches bending in the wind and halfway up was the moth.

The moth is already grown up, he thought. I don't have to wait for it a whole year. But it's gone away, like Maryanne has gone away.

Suddenly, as he remembered the moth, the idea came clear. He ran from the kitchen, up the stairs, and into his room.

CHAPTER NINE

Mark-o got out his crayons, paper, and paint set. First he drew a moth with white crayon on the white paper. Then he took blue water color and washed it over the whole page. When it dried, the moth stood out against the blue as though it were flying in the night.

He had learned how to make this kind of picture in school, but he had never done one by himself before. Now, as he looked at it, he thought it was the most beautiful picture he had ever seen. He could hardly believe he had done it. It made him sad, but it made him happy, too.

He raced downstairs with the picture and fastened it with Scotch tape to the wall at the back of a small table in the entryway. He could hardly work fast enough, he was in such a hurry. Then he ran to the jar with the cocoon and the cup of plants and set them on the table in front of the picture.

That afternoon, after school, Mark-O waited in the living room for Julie. Barbie came in first. When she saw the picture, she exclaimed, "Mark-O! Did you do that? It's beautiful! It looks like the moth . . ."

"It is," interrupted Mark-O. "Did you see it, too?"

"Oh, yes, and it startled me."

"How come?"

"I guess because it happened right when Maryanne died. It made me feel—well—like it was Maryanne."

Later, when Julie came in, the first thing *she* saw was the plant in the cup. "Oh, your seed is up! And look, there's the old dead seed on the leaf!"

"Yes," said Mark-O. "Barbie told me the seed had to crumble up so the plant inside could grow."

Then Julie pointed to the picture. "Is that the butter-fly out of your cocoon?"

"Yes, only it's a moth."

"Let's get some white paper," Julie said.

"For what?"

"You'll see." She and Mark-O went to his room to find the white paper. Julie cut a large square hole in the paper that just fitted the picture. She fastened it over the picture, which then had a white frame.

Julie stood looking at the picture after they had hung it back up. "You know," she said, "it looks like a fairy story picture—like a *magic* moth. I saw it, too, that night."

After a while, Stephen came in. The entryway was empty now. When he saw the picture, he stood a long while in front of it. Father came home while he was standing there.

"Dad, where do you suppose Mark-O got an idea like that?" Stephen asked.

"Mark-O's still young enough to ask questions and really look at things," said Father.

"I guess you got a point. Even if I do get tired of his questions sometimes." Stephen looked at the picture again.

Just then Mother came in from the kitchen to see who was talking in the front hall.

Father turned to her and said, "This picture of Mark-O's is unusual."

"I know," replied Mother. "And he has been so quiet

today—not at all himself. It *is* strange about that moth coming out of the cocoon when it did. Except that Maryanne seemed so cold that I had turned up the heat, and the room was unusually warm that evening. That could have done it, I suppose."

Barbie had been in the study showing Julie how to do an arithmetic problem. Hearing voices by the front door, they both came out to see what was happening.

"How long before dinner, Momma?" Julie asked.

"Nearly an hour," Mother replied. "The cake is still in the oven."

Mark-O came down from his room to find his whole family standing in front of his picture. It reminded him of the night they had all stood around Maryanne's bed to say good-bye, only there was a difference. They were not saying good-bye this time. They were beginning to remember Maryanne forever.

If Maryanne was here. Mark-O thought, she would make up the beginning of a story about my picture. It would go like this: "Once upon a time there was a caterpillar that spun a cocoon and one day . . ."

If you had looked in the dining room window of the George Foss home an hour later, you would have seen Father, Stephen, Barbie, Julie, and Mark-O sitting around the table finishing their dinner. It was the 9th of

March and Mother had just returned from the kitchen with a pale green cake sprinkled with peanuts.

"Oh!" screeched Mark-O. "It's my favorite cake!"

"Well, then, Mark-O, whose cake shall this be?" asked Mother.

Mark-O thought and thought.

"We've had all the guinea pigs," said Julie.

"And all the cats," said Barbie.

"And the dogs," said Stephen.

It's about time for Maryanne's birthday, thought Mark-O, but it made him feel bad so he did not say it aloud. He wondered if the others remembered.

Everyone was silent, waiting for Mark-O to decide on the birthday. The electric clock on the wall hummed loudly.

"I guess," said Mark-O finally, "that it's the moth's birthday."

"You made a good choice," said Father. "Now you may light the candle."

Mark-O had never been allowed to light a candle at the table and he felt very grand and important as he struck the match on the side of the box. It lit on the first strike, as though he had always lit candles for the cakes. Carefully, he held the match to the candle, then blew it out and laid it on his plate. He waited for someone to start singing "Happy Birthday," but no one did.

"I guess," said Father, "that we can't sing yet, but perhaps we will next year. Let's all blow the candle out together, instead."

Everyone took a huge breath and blew hard. The candle went out and Mother began to cut the cake. The first piece was a large one and she handed it to Mark-O.